Moving Day

PaRRagon

Bath · New York · Singapore · Hong Kong · Cologne · Delhi
Melbourne · Amsterdam · Johannesburg · Auckland · Shenzhen

Page 7

Pages 10-11

Page 11

Page 12

Page 16

Page 18-19

Page 19

Page 26

Page 28

Page 29

It's moving day! Sophia feels excited
about her new house, but a little sad, too.

Can you find these things in the picture?

FOR SALE

Kitchen

6

She will miss her old house and her best friend, Michael. He lives next door.

Michael comes to help Sophia finish her packing.
"I'll miss you!" he says.

He gives her a card and a gift. "Open it
when you get to your new house!"

Match these toys with their shadows.

Answer

Soon it is time to go. "Say good-bye to Michael," says Mom. "I don't want to go," Sophia says. "I'll have no one to play with."

Can you find these things in the picture?

"You'll make new friends," says Mom.
"And Michael can come to visit."

Place the sticker of Sophia here.

Sophia and her family follow the moving truck.
They stop at a restaurant for lunch.

Find 3 stickers to finish the picture.

12

Which two pieces finish the picture?

a.

b.

c.

d.

Answer   Pieces "a." and "d." finish the picture.

After a long drive, they reach the new house. Can you find five differences in the bottom picture?

SOLD

Answer

Sophia and her brother, Ryan, race off to explore the house.

"Let's choose our rooms!" shouts Ryan.

When Sophia and Ryan come back downstairs, the moving men are bringing in the furniture.

Find the sticker of Sophia to finish the picture.

Mom is busy unpacking boxes.
"Time for a break," says Dad.

Help Mom to unpack.
Point to the cabinet where each thing belongs.

Answer

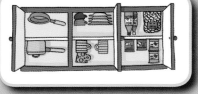

Sophia opens Michael's present.
It's a photograph. "I miss Michael," says Sophia.

Find 3 stickers to finish the picture.

Can you find these things in the picture?

Dad sees how sad she is. "Come on, let's go to the park for a while," he says.

Place the sticker of the photo here.

Help Sophia and her dad find their way to the park.

Answer

It's very quiet at the park. There's just Sophia and another little girl. Dad is talking to her mom.

Can you find 3 butterflies?

Which of these things begin with the letter b?

Answer

Bee, butterfly, bird, and baby all begin with the letter b.

23

The little girl asks Sophia if she wants to play.
"My name is Ava," she says.

Find the doll that matches Sophia's doll exactly.

a.

b.

c.

d.

e.

f.

Answer   Doll "f." matches.

When Sophia gets home, she tells her mom about Ava. "I hope I see her again," she says.

Join the pairs of shoes that go together. Which shoe doesn't have a pair?

Answer

The next day, Ava comes over with her mom and her baby brother. They have brought an apple pie to welcome Sophia's family.

How many crayons can you count?

Can you find these things in the picture?

28

Sophia and Ava play while the moms chat.
"I'm drawing a picture of you and me," says Ava.
"And I'm going to draw you!" says Sophia.

Find 2 stickers to finish the picture.

Place the sticker of Ava's picture here.

At bedtime, Sophia's mom sticks Ava's picture on the bedroom wall.

"I'm not sad about moving anymore," says Sophia happily, "because now I have two best friends!"